Theater Masters' Take Ten Volume VIII

9.5
by Emma Zetterberg

Crossover
by Zachariah Ezer

God and The Painter
by J.C. Pankratz

Imposter's Eve^{zzz}
by Malique Guinn

...in daylight
by DJ Hills

sleepover
by Alica Daine Benning

The Death Card
by Forest Malley

SAMUEL FRENCH

production are strongly advised to apply to the appropriate agent before starting rehearsals, advertising, or booking a theatre. A licensing fee must be paid whether the title(s) is presented for charity or gain and whether or not admission is charged. Professional/Stock licensing fees are quoted upon application to Concord Theatricals Corp.

This work is published by Samuel French, an imprint of Concord Theatricals Corp.

No one shall make any changes in this title(s) for the purpose of production. No part of this book may be reproduced, stored in a retrieval system, scanned, uploaded, or transmitted in any form, by any means, now known or yet to be invented, including mechanical, electronic, digital, photocopying, recording, videotaping, or otherwise, without the prior written permission of the publisher. No one shall share this title(s), or any part of this title(s), through any social media or file hosting websites.

For all inquiries regarding motion picture, television, online/digital and other media rights, please contact Concord Theatricals Corp.

MUSIC AND THIRD-PARTY MATERIALS USE NOTE

Licensees are solely responsible for obtaining formal written permission from copyright owners to use copyrighted music and/or other copyrighted third-party materials (e.g. artworks, logos) in the performance of this play and are strongly cautioned to do so. If no such permission is obtained by the licensee, then the licensee must use only original music and materials that the licensee owns and controls. Licensees are solely responsible and liable for clearances of all third-party copyrighted materials, including without limitation music, and shall indemnify the copyright owners of the play(s) and their licensing agent, Concord Theatricals Corp., against any costs, expenses, losses and liabilities arising from the use of such copyrighted third-party materials by licensees. For music, please contact the appropriate music licensing authority in your territory for the rights to any incidental music.

IMPORTANT BILLING AND CREDIT REQUIREMENTS

If you have obtained performance rights to this title, please refer to your licensing agreement for important billing and credit requirements.

THEATER MASTERS STAFF/BOARD

Victoria Hansen, Executive Artistic Director
Emily Zemba, Associate Artistic Director
Lulu Guzman, Artistic Administrator
Julia Hansen, Founder/Artistic Advisor

Advisory Board: Chris Ashley, Alec Baldwin, Andre Bishop, Scott Ellis, Doug Hughes, Judy Kaye, Andrew Leynse, John Lithgow, Robert Moss, Brian Murray, Jack O'Brien, Neil Pepe, Theresa Rebeck, John Rando, Tim Sanford, AR Gurney*, Gordon Davidson*

Board of Directors: Leyla Bader, Susan Buckley, Danielle Chock, Nancy Dunlap, Julia Hansen, Victoria Hansen, Gerri Karetsky, Marianne Lubar, Amy Rose Marsh, Naomi McDougall Jones, Sofia Milonas, Virginia Pearce, Jessica Salet, Nancy Stevens, Charlotte Tripplehorn, Daisy Walker

TAKE TEN 2022 CREATIVE TEAM

Kat Sloan Garcia, Stage Manager
Taylor Williams, CSA, Casting
Kari Buckley, Stage Directions
Edward T. Morris, Scenic Design

SPECIAL THANKS

Emily Dzioba, Stephen Cedars, Martyna Majok, Abbie Van Nostrand, Amy Rose Marsh, Ben Izzo, Max Grossman, Maria Striar, Michael Bulger, Aaron Malkin, Emily Morse, Mark Orsini, Bonnie Davis, Michael Walkup, Michael Finkle, Luke Virkstis, Emma Feiwel, Johnathan McRoy, Abe Koogler, Marvin Gonzale, Kate Tarker, James Anthony Tyler, Mary laws, RJ Tolan, Andrew Knight, Ralph Pena, Jeremy Cohen
...and so many more!

---

* emeritus

INTRODUCTION

Thank you for picking up the Take Ten Volume VIII, the collection of plays from Theater Masters' 2022 National MFA Playwrights Competition. This year's anthology includes seven short plays by playwrights from Boston University, Carnegie Mellon University, New York University, Northwestern University, UCLA, and UT Austin.

These seven Take Ten plays tackle the great themes of our time (Love, Spirituality, Identity, Revenge) with vulnerability, humor, and innovative theatricality. We believe these writers are the now and the future of the American Theater. We look forward to seeing their work grow and flourish beyond the pages of this anthology for many years to come.

Julia Hansen founded the National MFA Playwrights Competition and the Take Ten Festival in 2007 when she saw the need to bridge the gap between academic training and professional careers for emerging playwrights. For the past fifteen years, Take Ten's professional development opportunities and partnership with Concord Theatricals has provided playwrights with a career-igniting entrance into the entertainment industry, while introducing their voices to the landscape of the American theater.

For this year's virtual Take Ten, the winning playwrights joined us on Zoom for a packed week of industry meetings, panels, and one-on-one feedback sessions with working theater professionals – including our 2022 National Adjudicator, the Pulitzer Prize winning Martyna Majok. Our "Wonder Week" concluded with a virtual presentation of their work, directed by top new play directors: NJ Agwuna, victor cervantes jr, and Jessica Holt; featuring stunning scenic sketches by Edward T. Morris.

We would like to thank our donors, supportive Board of Directors, and the many artists, industry leaders, and Theater Masters' Alumni whose time and expertise helped to make Take Ten 2022 possible:

Emily Dzioba, Lulu Guzman, Stephen Cedars, Amy Rose Marsh & Abbie Van Nostrand (Concord Theatricals: Samuel French), Ben Izzo, Max Grossman, Michael Bulger & Maria Striar (Clubbed Thumb), Aaron Malkin (NYTW), Emily Morse (New Dramatists), Mark Orsini, Bonnie Davis, Michael Walkup (Page 73), Michael Finkle, Luke Virkstis, Emma Feiwel, Johnathan McRoy (National Black Theater), Abe Koogler, Marvin Gonzales, Kate Tarker, James Anthony Tyler, Mary laws, RJ Tolan (EST: Youngblood), Andrew Knight (South Coast Rep), Jeremy Cohen (The Playwrights Center), Taylor Williams (Taylor Williams Casting), Emmanuel Wilson (Dramatists Guild).

And finally: thank you for picking up this anthology and engaging with these intrepid theatrical voices.

Sincerely,

Vicky Hansen, Executive Artistic Director
Emily Zemba, Associate Artistic Director

TABLE OF CONTENTS

9.5

Emma Zetterberg

9.5 was first produced by Take Ten, a Virtual Ten Minute Play Festival on May 19th, 2022. The performance was directed by Jessica Holt. The cast was as follows:

CHRISTINA . . . . Emma Ramos
ROTH . . . . Steven Epp

CHARACTERS

CHRISTINA – before her prime, if she ever gets one
ROTH – past his prime, if he ever had one

SETTING

A patient's examination room at an OBGYN clinic. It's sterile and scary.

(AT RISE: **CHRISTINA** *walks into the fluorescent examination room of an OBGYN clinic.)*

(She takes off a winter coat. Underneath it she wears a white doctor's coat.)

*(***CHRISTINA*** takes a few instruments out of her coat pocket and lays them on the counter. Muttering to herself, preparing for the day.)*

(We hear a knock on the door.)

ROTH. Hello? May I come in?

CHRISTINA. One sec!

*(***CHRISTINA*** tears off her coat and jumps onto the examination table.)*

(Forgetting something, she takes out a pair of handcuffs from her coat pocket.)

(She shoves the handcuffs underneath the white sheet that she uses to cover her legs.)

*(***DR. ROTH*** enters. He doesn't glance at* **CHRISTINA** *as he flips through her medical records.)*

ROTH. Hi, I'm Dr. Roth. It looks like we've met before? Did you come in eight years ago? Were you seeing another doctor in between?

CHRISTINA. A few.

ROTH. Hmm, well you can ask them to share your records with us, so we have a better idea of how to treat you. Or has everything been going well?

(**CHRISTINA** *laughs.*)

So uh, what brings you in then? Sarah said we needed to squeeze you in before everyone, so I came in early.

CHRISTINA. I was going to thank her for getting me in, but it looks like she's not in yet.

ROTH. *(Yawning.)* No, she doesn't come in until 9. So, what's going on?

CHRISTINA. Well. I'm in pain.

ROTH. Okay...

CHRISTINA. A lot of pain.

ROTH. Is this pain around your period?

CHRISTINA. It used to be.

Now it's all the time.

(*He starts scribbling on a prescription pad.*)

ROTH. Okay we'll get you started on birth control. That can help thin out the endometrial lining – which is what sheds every month when you have your menses. That'll help with what we call Dysmenorrhea – which is the medical term for pain during menstruation.

CHRISTINA. Oh I forgot. I already have an IUD. The Mirena.

ROTH. This is why we need your records from the other offices.

CHRISTINA. I suppose, but I wanted your second opinion, and I thought it might be better if we go at it from square one. Just so nothing influences your diagnosis, except you.

ROTH. ...Fine. Where is it hurting?

CHRISTINA. Mostly here. But also here. And sometimes here. And sometimes I feel like there's little electric shocks running through my Vagina. Like Vag lightning.

(Beat. Vag lightning??)

ROTH. If you're on the IUD then it could be possible that it's come out of place – punctured the uterine wall. Or an ovarian cyst.

CHRISTINA. Already got an ultrasound. Everything's fine.

ROTH. *(Growing exasperated.)* Okay do you have the ultrasound report?

CHRISTINA. Yup.

ROTH. Here?

CHRISTINA. There's nothing to note. Are you going to look at the images? Or just read the report? My ovaries are 4.2 centimeters wide. My Endometrium is 4.4 millimeters. The Endometrial stripe is within normal limits. "Nothing abnormal to report."

Believe me. I've read it a million times, trying to find something that could explain it, but nothing does. Except well...I was looking around online. I heard about this thing called Endometriosis. Could it be that?

ROTH. It's unlikely.

CHRISTINA. I heard it won't show up on ultrasounds.

ROTH. Yes, but if you're in as much pain as you say you are, then it probably would show something. How long has your pain been going on? A few weeks?

CHRISTINA. Eight years.

ROTH. And always at this level? Which is, what level would you say it is out of 10?

CHRISTINA. A 10.

ROTH. 10 would be screaming, crying – well not even, it would be passing out from the pain.

CHRISTINA. Fine. A 9.5.

ROTH. Okay so you've been experiencing a 9.5 level of pain for eight years and you've only come to see me *now*?

CHRISTINA. I saw you eight years ago.

ROTH. Look when it comes to your body, you have to be proactive. Come in if it's bothering you. Then we don't have to squeeze you in early in the morning before nurses are even in the office.

CHRISTINA. Sorry. So what do I do now?

(He pulls on a pair of gloves.)

ROTH. Well, I'll give you a physical examination. I'm going to press in different areas, you tell me where and how much it hurts.

CHRISTINA. I already told you. It's a 9.5, here, here, and here. You don't have to –

ROTH. Look if it's really bothering you then I do. Breathe out, relax your stomach muscles. Can you lift up your shirt?

> (**CHRISTINA** *lies back on the table, sliding one hand underneath the sheet.*)

CHRISTINA. No.

ROTH. *(Sighing.)* Well, it won't be as thorough this way, but

> *(He presses down and she screams – a long, ululating cry.)*

> (**ROTH** *tries to pull away, but he is now <u>handcuffed</u> to the table.*)

WHAT THE HELL!

CHRISTINA. I told you it was a 9.5. I told you! I told you eight years ago. I came in screaming. Shaking. I was bleeding so much. Like someone turned on the tap, it was pouring out of me. I would pee and more blood than pee would come out. No one can bleed that much and be okay. I thought I was going to die. And I was screaming, telling you I was going to die.

And then the moment I told you I was on SSRI's, you dismissed me. Do you know what you diagnosed it as? A panic attack. And Dysmenorrhea. An anxious woman with painful periods. You told me and I quote, "You know, sometimes periods can be uncomfortable."

Yeah I KNOW. How do YOU know?? Does this look like I'm uncomfortable? Does this look normal?

ROTH. Okay, Okay! Just calm down. We'll figure it out. Together. Just. Please unlock this.

(**CHRISTINA** *puts on her white doctor's coat.*)

CHRISTINA. Diagnose me first. If you get it right then sure.

ROTH. We should rule out an ovarian cyst.

CHRISTINA. Ruled out. Ovaries are normal on the ultrasound.

ROTH. Appendix.

CHRISTINA. Normal.

ROTH. Ectopic pregnancy.

CHRISTINA. I just told you the ultrasound was normal.

ROTH. Okay, okay. Fibroids?

CHRISTINA. No. Well, there was a tiny fibroid but it was removed. C'mon, is your memory that bad? I literally told you about it earlier.

ROTH. You know, the thing is Endometriosis is really hard to diagnose.

CHRISTINA. Why?

ROTH. Because it's when your uterine lining grows outside of your uterus. And that lining thickens over the span of your cycle and then bleeds. And whenever there's anything in your abdomen – liquid or whatever, that isn't supposed to be there, it can cause a lot of pain. BUT. But you said you're in pain <u>every day</u>. Well, with Endometriosis that pain is usually *cyclical.* Going along with your cycle.

Plus the only way to confirm it is with surgery. Which I usually don't recommend because why get cut up if you don't have to, might as well try birth control, which is less invasive first and see where that goes –

CHRISTINA. I've done birth control. SO many kinds. It doesn't work. It makes you depressed. Makes you feel crazy. I'm not crazy, or at least I wasn't before. Just gained weight. Lost weight. Got stretch marks.

ROTH. Okay. If it's surgery you want then fine, we can do that. Please, can you unlock this and I can look at my schedule to get you in –

CHRISTINA. What does the surgery look like?

ROTH. Well it's laparoscopic. So as minimally invasive as possible. We put a needle through your belly button and fill your stomach up with air so we can cut through and not hit anything else. Then we'll do three other incisions for different tools – one of which is a camera. And we go have a look.

CHRISTINA. And if you find it?

ROTH. Then we burn it out with a laser.

CHRISTINA. *Burn it out?*

ROTH. Yes. It's called Ablation. And I know that sounds scary, which is why I recommend trying other treatments first.

<table>
<tr><td>ROTH.</td><td>CHRISTINA.</td></tr>
<tr><td>There are studies that even apple cider vinegar –</td><td>If you say apple cider vinegar, I will kill you.</td></tr>
</table>

ROTH. You're...joking right?

CHRISTINA. Only if you are. Were you joking?

> (**CHRISTINA** *lifts up her shirt to reveal four bandages.*)

It was confirmed. Twice.

The thing is, if you do ablation, what happens is you burn the top of the tissue, but the bottom just grows deeper into your flesh. Like mold. Do you ever buy strawberries and find one with a bit of mold?

I asked you a question.

ROTH. Yes. Yeah sure.

CHRISTINA. Well what do you do?

ROTH. Umm, I either throw the strawberry out.

CHRISTINA. Or?

ROTH. Or I cut off the moldy part.

CHRISTINA. Have you ever thought you cut all of it out, and just taken a bite of that nasty strawberry, and tasted the rancid shit on your tongue that tells you YOU DIDN'T GET ALL OF IT OUT???

Because they didn't get all of it out. After eight years of bouncing from doctor to doctor, I finally got that surgery. The first one. The ablation. And it worked, for a bit. And two months later – when I had finally recovered from having my stomach cut open, the pain came back. Slowly at first. But within six months I was back to where I was before. 9.5. *9.5!*

They told me that sometimes it's just your nerve endings. When they've been sending the pain signal for so long, they don't know how to stop. So, I thought maybe it was all in my head? Maybe it actually wasn't that bad? Maybe everyone feels this way? Right?

CHRISTINA. And then I found a specialist. My holy grail. A rock star doctor who specialized in Endo and only Endo. Of course, he was out of state and my insurance wouldn't cover the surgery. Do you want to know how much it cost? Guess.

ROTH. Seven thousand.

CHRISTINA. It was ten thousand. Just for his physician fee. And then the hospital he operated out of charged me another eight.

ROTH. Do you want money? Is that what you're here for? I'll give it to you. Please.

CHRISTINA. I didn't have the money so I took the debt. Because if this surgery worked. I could go back to normal. But when they opened me up, they saw the mold everywhere. It was never fully cut out. So it grew back. And because the top of it had been burned to a crisp it had no choice but to grow <u>deeper</u> into my flesh.

What was the first thing you said you do to a moldy strawberry?

ROTH. ...throw it out.

CHRISTINA.   And that's what had to happen. Full hysterectomy.

Nothing's growing down there. Not even a weed.

(Beat.)

ROTH. I'm sorry.

CHRISTINA. I would like to say it's not your fault. But I do wonder...What would've happened if you had listened? But more importantly, what has already happened because you *didn't*?

And not just to me.

> (**CHRISTINA** *picks up a scalpel from the table.*)

ROTH. What are you going to do with that?

CHRISTINA. Do you know how many people with ovaries have endometriosis?

ROTH. No.

CHRISTINA. No? *No?* It's one in ten. How many patients will you see before lunch today?

ROTH. Maybe 20.

CHRISTINA. And after?

ROTH. Depends how late I'm working.

CHRISTINA. Guess.

ROTH. I don't know. 20.

CHRISTINA. Okay so that's four people a day with Endo that, well let's be honest, with your medical *expertise*, are going undiagnosed. Four people like me a day. That's twenty each week. A thousand each year. Give or take. And that's just you. You're just one. single. OBGYN.

Letting down *one thousand* women each year.

So you understand why I'm doing this, right? I need to save them. They need help.

> (**CHRISTINA** *approaches him with a scalpel, preparing to strike his belly.*)

ROTH. No. NO. NO Please! PLEASE! I'm SORRY. I'm SORRY. I FUCKED UP. I DIDN'T KNOW ANY BETTER. IT'S NOT LIKE WE'RE TAUGHT THIS. NO ONE KNOWS ANYTHING ABOUT ENDOMETRIOSIS. THEY DON'T EVEN KNOW WHAT CAUSES IT. AND THAT *IS* UNFAIR TO...to – um, to you...

CHRISTINA. You don't remember my name, do you?

ROTH. I see so many people every day. I'm tired. I don't always remember. My job is hard, too.

CHRISTINA. Right. I'm tired too. And I know it's difficult. I know that you do probably help some of your patients. So, tell me one of their names.

ROTH. I'm stressed, I can't remember.

CHRISTINA. I am Christina.

Now you are Christina too.

> *(She thrusts the scalpel deep into him.)*

> *(He screams – blood curdling. And blood does curdle as it pours out of him.)*

ROTH. Oh GOD. OH GOD. HELP.

> (**ROTH** *continues to whimper underneath* **CHRISTINA***'s lines.)*

CHRISTINA. But there's something beautiful about pain. It reminds you that it's real. It drives you crazy but keeps you from going over the edge. This isn't in your head, is it?

ROTH. No.

CHRISTINA. It's real?

ROTH. Yes.

> (**CHRISTINA** *sighs in relief.)*

> *(Almost lovingly, she puts some blood on his cheeks, drawing two clown circles of blush and painting his lips red.)*

CHRISTINA. Some blush on your cheeks. A little rouge on your lips. Now you know what it's like to be me.

(**CHRISTINA** *begins to gather her things.*)

ROTH. Please GOD. Please somebody help me. I can't do this. Ohh it hurts. My lips are going numb. I can't feel my lips. So much blood. MOM? MOM. Oh I'm going to die. Oh god I'm going to die. HELP. PLEASE.

(*He screams – a long, ululating cry.* **CHRISTINA** *freezes.*)

CHRISTINA. Stop that. No please. Stop that. Shh. Shh.

(*She holds* **DR. ROTH** *in her arms.*)

It'll be okay, Christina. I've got you.

You'll be okay. You'll be okay,

We'll fix it. Together.

Crossover

Zachariah Ezer

CROSSOVER was first produced by Take Ten, a Virtual Ten Minute Play Festival on May 19th, 2022. The performance was directed by victor cervantes jr. The cast was as follows:

JO. . . . . Simone Immanuel

HAMM. . . . . Je'Shaun Aukeem Jackson

AMIRAN/THE YESHAP. . . . . Esco Jouley

THE NARRATOR. . . . . Brandon Gill

CHARACTERS

JO – Black Woman
HAMM – Genderless Black Person
AMIRAN – Black Man
THE YESHAP – Monster
THE NARRATOR – Black Stan Lee

AUTHOR'S NOTES

The freezes when The Narrator speaks should be staged like comic book panels.

Amiran and The Yeshap may be doubled. The Narrator may be prerecorded.

(Lights up on **JO**, *a Black woman in a tattered robe, holding a blade to the neck of* **HAMM**, *a Black non-binary person wearing the same.)*

HAMM. You must kill me! It's the only way!

JO. After everything we've been through, how could I even think about it?

*(**JO** and **HAMM** freeze.)*

("Outlandish Fantasy #70" is projected above them, turning their tableau into a comic book cover tableau.)

(We hear the disembodied voice of **THE NARRATOR**.*)*

THE NARRATOR. Hey there, true believers! You picked a hell of a time to drop in. I'm sure you got a thousand questions, like "Why is that lady about to kill that non-binary person?" "Who the hell is talking to me right now?" And "What gives? I thought this was a play, not some kinda cheap comic book." Well, all those questions, and more, will be answered, but first, we gotta go back to the beginning.

(Blackout.)

*(Lights up on **HAMM**, seated on a rock, reading a Superman comic.)*

*(**HAMM** freezes.)*

THE NARRATOR. Have you ever wondered how white people happened? It's important; I promise. The legend goes that some Brahman Indians – *(That's the whitest kind of Indians, for those of you not in the know.)* – traveled north through the perilous peaks of the Caucasus Mountains. When they came out, they were as pale as the snow on the mountaintops. With their newfound whiteness, they were ready to ruin the world as we know it! As they colonized the globe, word soon spread, and people learned that all you had to do to become white was walk the same trail as the Brahmans. Many have tried, but few have succeeded. Join me in witnessing one such attempt in today's story: "Outlandish Fantasy #70: Through the Mountain Pass."

*(**HAMM** unfreezes. **JO** enters carrying a satchel. Both freeze.)*

That's Sojourner Truth. You met her before when we covered her escape from slavery in "Too Good To Be Fake #97." She's an abolitionist; she's a feminist; hell, she's an all-around hero, but for now, everyone just calls her Jo.

*(**JO** and **HAMM** unfreeze.)*

JO. Is this the end of the road?

HAMM. In a manner of speaking.

JO. I mean, is this where I'm supposed to wait?

HAMM. Wait for what?

*(**JO** looks around furtively before answering.)*

JO. *(Whispering.)* To become white.

HAMM. Sorry, what was that?

(**JO** *sighs.*)

JO. To become white.

HAMM. You shouldn't believe everything you hear.

JO. *(Gesturing to the comic book.)* What about what you read?

(**HAMM** *puts the comic book down.*)

HAMM. You shouldn't believe a word of that.

JO. So, are you waiting too?

HAMM. I certainly am.

JO. How long have you been here? I didn't see you on the path ahead of me.

HAMM. Hard to say. Things are strange here; time doesn't run the way it does elsewhere.

JO. Ain't that the truth! I can't tell if I've been walking an hour or a week. *(Beat.)* Jo.

HAMM. Nice to meet you.

JO. This is the part where, typically, you would tell me your name.

HAMM. I suppose it is, isn't it?

JO. Fair enough. We've all got our reasons to keep to ourselves.

(**JO** *sits near* **HAMM.**)

HAMM. Why do you wish to become white, Jo?

JO. So, which is it? Are you secretive or chatty?

HAMM. It depends on the topic.

JO. Then consider this one where I'm not chatty.

HAMM. Fair enough.

(**HAMM** *goes back to reading the comic book.* **JO** *watches them a moment.*)

JO. Can I ask what you're reading?

HAMM. It's about a man who hides his true self from the rest of the world so that he can help them.

JO. Sounds like a bunch of bullshit to me.

HAMM. This from someone looking to change their race?

JO. If I could help people as me, I'd do it.

HAMM. Most of us have more power than we think.

JO. I think I'd like to sit in silence again.

(*They do, but only for a moment. The ground shakes.*)

What is that?

HAMM. The first trial.

JO. Trial?

(**JO** *and* **HAMM** *freeze.*)

THE NARRATOR. Jo doesn't know it, but the Brahmans have made turning white a little harder than when they did it. Talk about pulling the ladder up behind you! They set up three trials, starting with The Yeshap, a six-armed beast they enslaved who requires a bribe in order to let travelers pass. Otherwise, it tears them limb from limb and eats them alive!

(**JO** *and* **HAMM** *unfreeze.* **THE YESHAP** *enters, covered in hair and scratching furiously.* **JO** *stands.*)

JO. Sweet Jesus.

THE YESHAP. What have you brought me, mortal?

JO. I, uh…I'm not sure.

THE YESHAP. Bad news for you, because I am hungry.

JO. *(Gesturing to* **HAMM.***)* What about them? Can't they go first?

(**THE YESHAP** *scoffs, still scratching.)*

THE YESHAP. I cannot eat one who has been cursed. It is forbidden.

JO. Cursed? So you're not here to become white?

(**HAMM** *keeps reading, pretending not to hear.)*

THE YESHAP. My offering. Now.

JO. Gimme a second here, let me just check my bag.

THE YESHAP. Your bag? I have killed kings and clerics for bringing me gold and salvation. What could you possibly have in your peasant's rucksack that would satisfy me?

(**JO** *rummages through her bag. She looks up at* **THE YESHAP,** *scratching as if its life depended on it.)*

(*She pulls out a simple wooden comb.)*

What is this?

JO. You look itchy. I thought it might help.

(**THE YESHAP** *roughly grabs the comb from* **JO.** *It begins scratching itself with the comb.)*

THE YESHAP. Oh, yes!

JO. You like that?

THE YESHAP. This will do nicely, mortal. You may continue your quest.

(**THE YESHAP** *exits, furiously scratching itself with the comb as it goes.*)

HAMM. *(Without looking up.)* Well done.

JO. No thanks to you.

(**HAMM** *looks at* **JO.**)

HAMM. How did you know The Yeshap would respond to the comb?

JO. My son. He came down from the Big House scratching like that one day, like he was trying to take his skin off. Like he'd do anything to stop the itch. He'd never had lice before, but someone up there must have given 'em to him. I had to comb his hair all night to get them out.

HAMM. Your son? Is he why you –

JO. *(Deflecting.)* – So, what's this about you being cursed?

HAMM. By my father.

(**JO** *and* **HAMM** *freeze.*)

THE NARRATOR. For more on that curse, check out "Genesis #925."

(**JO** *and* **HAMM** *unfreeze.*)

JO. Why would he do that?

HAMM. I saw him in sin, and now, I cannot leave this place.

JO. So, are you like a guide?

HAMM. Jo, you are ill-prepared for this journey, and there are secrets hidden in these mountains that you are better off not knowing. I highly advise you leave now.

JO. I can't do that. Not yet. I didn't come all this way to go home empty-handed.

HAMM. You mean you won't go home Black?

JO. I know you're not on the same path I am, but that doesn't mean you get to judge me.

(*A moment. The stage lights dim.*)

HAMM. My apologies.

JO. That's better.

(**JO** *pulls a lantern from her bag.*)

HAMM. What are you doing?

JO. It's getting dark. I'm going to need some light.

HAMM. You can't do that. You'll hasten the second trial.

JO. I knew it! You are a guide.

HAMM. I am not a guide.

JO. So you're saying you don't give everyone advice on how to get through the trials?

HAMM. No! I just...I want you to get a fair shot at completing them, especially since you don't even know what they are.

JO. Sure. Well, I'm trying to finish as soon as possible, and, no offense, but I don't know how much longer I wanna be hanging around here.

(**JO** *sits down and turns on her lantern. She pulls out a piece of paper and studies it.*)

HAMM. Can I ask what you're reading?

(*A moment.*)

JO. I'm working on a speech. (*Beat.*) There's a convention for women in Akron, Ohio.

HAMM. I see.

JO. Do you know Akron?

HAMM. I don't. Is it safe for...

JO. ...For Black folks? Nowhere in this world is safe for Us, but it's a free state if that's what you mean.

HAMM. If the state is free, then why do you need to be white?

JO. I can't do everything I gotta do in free states.

HAMM. What do you want to do?

JO. I told you, I'm not talking about my –

HAMM. – I don't mean the big thing. Something small.

(**JO** *thinks a moment.*)

JO. Pork belly.

HAMM. What?

JO. I'd eat some pork belly. Don't get me wrong, I love chitlins, but I've always been curious what they do with the part of the pig they take before they give it to Us, and ain't nowhere up north got good soul food.

HAMM. I see.

JO. What about you?

(**HAMM** *is surprised.*)

HAMM. You know, no one has ever asked me before. *(Beat.)* I would see the world. I've never left the Caucasus, at least not since there's been an Akron, Ohio.

JO. How old are you?

HAMM. I –

AMIRAN. *(From offstage.)* – Mom?

JO. Did you hear that?

(**HAMM** *nods.*)

AMIRAN. *(From offstage.)* Mom, where are you? I'm scared.

JO. Peter? Is that you?

> (**AMIRAN**, *a Black man in a tattered robe, enters, appearing fearful.* **HAMM** *looks surprised to see him.*)

HAMM. Amiran? Is that *you*?

AMIRAN. Mom, I wanna go home.

HAMM. Jo, that is not your son! It's not real.

> (**JO** *and* **HAMM** *freeze.* **AMIRAN** *does not.*)

THE NARRATOR. They're right. Amiran is a trickster. He used to be the hero of the Caucasus mountains. He robbed god of his fire so he could share it with the mortals. Pretty swell guy. Well, for his transgression, he was chained to a rock. Now, every day a dog eats his heart, and it turns him evil at night. But can you blame him? I'd be pretty irritable myself. And if that wasn't bad enough, he was sold to the Brahmans. Now, he appears to travelers as the one they love most and lures them to their deaths in the fire to try and earn his freedom. But try telling Jo that.

> (**JO** *and* **HAMM** *unfreeze.*)

JO. Quiet, I need to take a look at my boy.

> (**AMIRAN** *stands in front of the lantern. The fire seems to grow.* **JO** *inspects him.*)

AMIRAN. Mom, come hold me.

> (**JO** *puts her face directly next to* **AMIRAN**'s.)

JO. You are not my Peter.

AMIRAN. Mom, please, by the fire. It's so cold up here.

JO. I have no idea what you are, but I know that you are no kin of mine.

AMIRAN. Mom, I love you. Please don't leave me again.

 (**JO** *chokes up. She looks as if she is going to give in, but she turns her body away from* **AMIRAN**.*)*

JO. You have no power over me, demon.

 (**AMIRAN***'s body language changes, becoming less human. He throws a tantrum. The fire rages.)*

AMIRAN. You stupid bitch! I will burn you alive! You too, Cursed One! You'll not see the morning!

 (**AMIRAN** *continues to rage, but it is impotent. Soon, he and the fire disappear. As soon as they do,* **JO** *breaks.)*

HAMM. You do not know the trials, Jo. How could you tell he was not your son?

JO. My son was whipped recently. *(Beat.)* I got a letter telling me his face had been scarred. I have not seen it yet.

HAMM. So Amiran was unable to appear to you as your son is now.

 (**HAMM** *moves closer to console* **JO**.*)*

JO. I feel like I am losing my mind up here.

HAMM. I am so sorry, Jo. Is he –

JO. – Yes, he's why I want to be white. He was stolen from me, and this is the only way that I can get him back without being enslaved again myself.

HAMM. I see.

 (**HAMM** *gets on their knees and pulls a dagger from their clothes. They attempt to hand it to* **JO**.*)*

HAMM. Then you must kill me.

JO. Kill you? What are you talking about? Why would I kill you?

HAMM. Because it is my fault you lost your son. Because I am the reason you have suffered your entire life. Because that is the third trial.

JO. What? Why?

HAMM. Because, Jo, I am The First One. I am Hamm.

(**JO** and **HAMM** *freeze.*)

THE NARRATOR. That's right, true believers! Jo's guide has been the biblical Hamm all along! Wait, you don't know who Hamm is? Are you sure? (*Sighs.*) Kids these days. Okay, so maybe you know their poppa, Noah? The ark? Two of every animal? Flood for about six weeks? Okay, great. Well, that ark had to land somewhere. It found rest at Mt. Ararat, the highest peak where, do you think? Ding, ding, ding! That's right, the Caucasus. Give the kid a prize. Well, once Noah and the family got settled, he decided someone had to do all the dirty work. He tried to enslave his own family, and for daring to stand up to him, Hamm and their progeny were cursed forever. Their wife, Na-El, soon fled the mountains, but she was with child, and she spread the curse throughout the Earth. And that's how Black people happened, or so they say.

(**JO** *and* **HAMM** *unfreeze.*)

JO. I thought Noah only had sons.

HAMM. I am that I am. Blackness troubles gender.

JO. Why tell me this?

HAMM. You did not bribe the Yeshap, you helped it. Amiran did not appear as some king or god or businessman; he appeared to you as the child you are trying to save. You are what I have been waiting for, Jo: someone worthy of breaking this curse for both of us. Get what you came here for. Get your son.

> (**HAMM** *holds out the knife again.* **JO** *grabs it this time. She holds it to* **HAMM**'s *throat.* **JO** *and* **HAMM** *freeze.*)

THE NARRATOR. And we're back to our pulse-pounding climax. Will Jo kill Hamm to regain custody of her son? Will killing Hamm make Jo white forever? Will you ever learn who I really am? Find out next issue in "Outlandish Fantasy #71."

> (*Blackout.*)

I'm just kidding. Who could cut away at a time like this?

*(Lights up on **JO** and **HAMM**. They unfreeze. **JO** throws the knife offstage.)*

HAMM. Why?

JO. We're leaving.

HAMM. I cannot.

JO. I know your curse. I heard nothing about you being forced to remain here.

HAMM. *(Gesturing to themselves.)* I cannot live in the world like this.

JO. You mean you won't live in it if you have to be Black? Why not? I do it every day.

HAMM. I am not strong enough.

*(**JO** pulls **HAMM** to their feet.)*

JO. Most of us have more power than we think.

HAMM. Jo, I –

JO. – I'm going to Akron, Ohio to get some pork belly, and you're coming with me.

(A long moment. The stage lights come back up.)

HAMM. I am.

JO. Good. Come on.

HAMM. Jo, how will you help your son?

JO. I will show them my true self. It got me this far. That is all any of Us can do.

(They both exit. Hold on the bare stage a moment.)

THE NARRATOR. Jo and Hamm ride off into the sunset... for now. But will she get her son back? There's only one way to find out. As the old expression goes, see you in the funny pages. Excelsior!

(Blackout.)

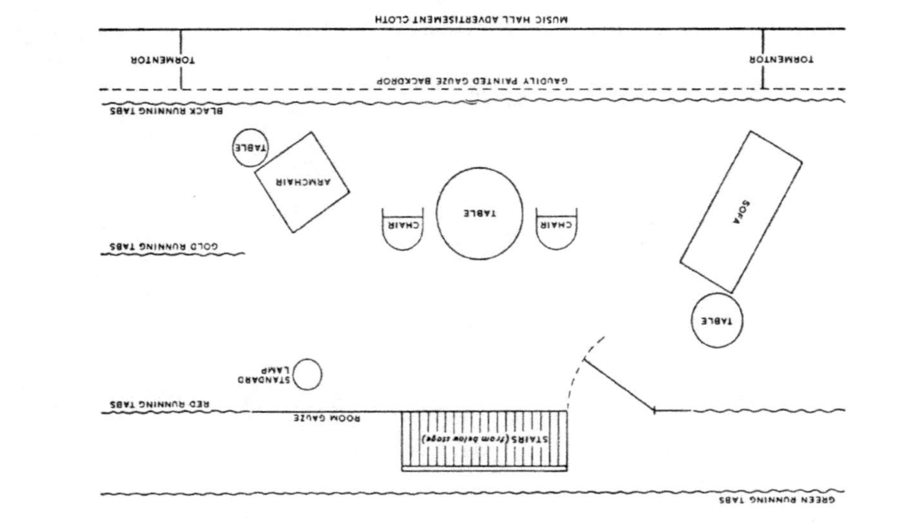

GREEN RUNNING TABS
RED RUNNING TABS
ROOM GAUZE
STANDARD LAMP
STAIRS (from below stage)
GOLD RUNNING TABS
TABLE
CHAIR
ARMCHAIR
TABLE
CHAIR
SOFA
TABLE
BLACK RUNNING TABS
GAUDILY PAINTED GAUZE BACKDROP
MUSIC HALL ADVERTISEMENT CLOTH
TORMENTOR
TORMENTOR

God and The Painter

J.C. Pankratz

GOD AND THE PAINTER was first produced by Take Ten, a Virtual Ten Minute Play Festival on May 19th, 2022. The performance was directed by victor cervantes jr. The cast was as follows:

GOD . . . . Pooya Mosheni

JAMIE . . . . B Norwood

CHARACTERS

GOD – a genderless cloud, any age.
JAMIE – a young painter, late twenties, any gender.

SETTING

A musty art studio.

TIME

Evening.

AUTHOR'S NOTES

God should not bear any resemblance to the ancient, white-bearded man we know from Renaissance paintings.

(Night in the studio. A giant canvas sits, immovable and pale. It sucks up all the light in the room the same way black velvet can. It is endless, and impossible, and utterly possible all at once.)

*(**JAMIE** stands, working open a bucket of paint on a stool with a paintkey.)*

*(**GOD**, a cloud, perches and watches. They are fluid, a changeling reflecting and transforming as light catches every facet of their form. Perhaps their face is made of jewels. Perhaps their steps make soft dead patches in the ground. Perhaps they have mammoth tusks. Perhaps their breath smells like beef jerky and rain. They're **GOD**, after all.)*

*(The paint can is open. **JAMIE** stands in front of the canvas, and hesitates just a moment too long.)*

GOD. Should I pose?

JAMIE. Uhh no, no thanks.

GOD. But *can* I?

JAMIE. If it suits you.

*(**GOD** drapes themself over a chair. Beat.)*

GOD. You're not even looking!!

JAMIE. You hurt my eyes.

I have to do this sort of – peripheral vision head tilt move.

GOD. Too bright?

JAMIE. You look like a migraine.

Exactly like a migraine, actually. A big floating shimmery amoeba.

> (**GOD** *opens their mouth and a spout of glitter erupts.*)

I wish you were a migraine

GOD. *(Kicks feet.)* Paint me.

JAMIE. I can say no, right?

GOD. Sure. But will you?

> (**JAMIE** *doesn't answer, dips a brush in the paint. Just before hesitation sets in, brush touches canvas. They paint a broad, curved line.*)

I'm not a line.

> (**JAMIE** *lets the curved line become a circle.*)

I'm not a circle.

Don't be boring!

Everyone else is wrong, or boring, or sometimes both.

This is both, just in case you're wondering.

> (**JAMIE** *rips the canvas away with startling force. There's another behind it, waiting and blank.*)

JAMIE. Stop posing.

GOD. *(Sits up.)* Okay! What should I do?

JAMIE. Show me your face.

GOD. Whaaat do you think this is?

JAMIE. It's not a face, it's – decor.

My mom always went to the doctor with a full face of makeup. She wanted to set the atmosphere. As though you can give liver cancer a first impression.

GOD. She felt gracious, and powerful, and like all the odds were in her favor. It's why you put little rhinestones on your eyelashes before you leave to teach. And steam your silk pillowcases before you redownload the Grindr app on your iPhone.

JAMIE. I mean, I know –

Don't do that.

GOD. Do what.

JAMIE. Make this a thing about me when we're talking about you and painting you and you expect a whole portrait without showing me your face.

GOD. My face is right here, bud.

JAMIE. All I see is layers. Glitter and brimstone and untouchable bleak majesty.

GOD. Thank you

JAMIE. When you come you're a burning bush, or a bright light, or an angel, or a VERY LARGE CLOUD or or a bunch of fire, or, I don't know, other stuff, but –

I Know My Shit.

And I'm not painting until you're real.

GOD. My visage is too much for the people.

JAMIE. What do you see when you look in the mirror?

GOD. What everyone else sees, I guess

JAMIE. And that is...

GOD. All the faces of the living. All the faces of the dead. The broken crags of wrinkled earth. Pitted meteoric acne, the smooth cheeks of the oceans, the stubble of burned down forest.

JAMIE. Dandruff snow?

GOD. An Everest of eczema.

> *(All this time, **JAMIE** has been inching closer and closer.)*

JAMIE. Sounds like a lot.

GOD. Eons of suffering, of impossible joy. The newness of snake scales, fresh spring mud, hot corn tortillas – *HEY!*

> *(**JAMIE** reaches out and yanks, pulling off a piece of **GOD**'s mantle, whatever it is. Maybe just a feather. A tuft of cloud. A gem, a ribbon. Whatever it is, **JAMIE** holds it in their hand.)*

JAMIE. I knew it.

GOD. YOU JUST PULLED OFF A PIECE OF ME.

JAMIE. *I knew it.*

GOD. Fuck you, Jamie.

JAMIE. You said, "A real face, the real me, I promise."

GOD. Just kick me out next time, okay? Don't touch my ESSENCE.

You piece of shit. If you get to say no, I get to say no.

Even stevens.

JAMIE. But you're GOD. You're G O D.

There's no even stevens. Not even close.

You could lose your balance and fall off that chair and obliterate my apartment.

GOD. I'm careful .

JAMIE. I'm sorry, with what!? With what?!

Let's not get into literally everything you've ever done.

GOD. I get it. You're intimidated –

JAMIE. – Nooo, no no no, I'm not –

GOD. *(Louder.)* You're intimidated and I'm difficult, okay, but we can agree. This is the rule. The mutual no. Okay?

JAMIE. Yes. Okay. I'm sorry for snatching.

GOD. Forgiven.

I'm ready again.

JAMIE. Why do you want to be painted?

GOD. Who doesn't?

JAMIE. You have hundreds, if not thousands, of paintings.

GOD. They're wrong, or boring, or both.

JAMIE. I just don't see how I won't repeat it. I just –

(Cue epiphany.)

Oh. Oh.

GOD. Do I smell a hint of brilliance? A fart of phantasm?

JAMIE. I get it now. It's for you.

GOD. Hmm?

JAMIE. Charlton Heston's Ten Commandments – that dude becomes old in a millisecond because God gives him the tablets. It's bad to look at God. So we get a bush, a cloud, a flame, a – whatever. Too big, too bright, too much – if I see you, I become dust. It's over. My face melts off.

*(**GOD**: makes a small explosion sound.)*

JAMIE. But I bet – I bet my whole life – if you took away the fire, the glimmer, all of it. I bet we could look eye to eye.

GOD. You really wanna bet?

JAMIE. Actually, I do.

(*Sits.*)

It's not about protecting us. It's about hiding you.

We all live in the pit of your stomach and you're afraid to look down in case we catch a glimpse of the Divine Master.

GOD. What a boring theory.

JAMIE. Why do you want to be painted?

GOD. I like seeing other interpretations.

JAMIE. So you want to see my interpretation of your interpretation of...yourself.

GOD. Isn't it all the same?

JAMIE. Sure. I don't mean to say –

(*A long quiet.*)

My mom grew up in the middle of nowhere, butter and sugar sandwich poor. And when I say her mom told her all she had was a face, I mean it. Nobody had the heart to indulge her in what she really wanted, you know? Her hopes or dreams or whatever. It was their kind of love. You have to be tough when disappointment is the salt at the table.

(*They clear their throat.*)

She was Rembrandt, straight up. Every dash of color and powder, every little slide of mascara was planned, and practiced, and completed with perfect muscle memory. She knew exactly what she looked like all the time. Never saw her without it. Perfect self-portraiture.

GOD. So?

JAMIE. I remember – in hospice, coming in early with some flowers for her room, and stopping in the hallway because I didn't expect her to be awake. She was putting on makeup. No mirror. Eyeshadow, eyeliner, mascara, blush, lipstick. And when she was done blotting she –

> (**JAMIE** *tilts forward in their seat slowly, so slowly.*)

She leaned forward. Like the weight of the continent was resting on the back of her neck. Like her face was stone. And then I saw on the blanket she was crying. She was leaning like that so her tears fell straight down, and didn't mess up her face.

> (**JAMIE** *stays leaned into the position, in the memory, until they can lean back into themselves.*)

Part of it was dignity. Part of it was choice. And part of it was – I don't think she knew how to stop. Or who she was without it. It was all the same for her, too.

GOD. I don't remember what I look like.

JAMIE. What?

GOD. I don't remember what I look like. I don't actually know if I know.

JAMIE. You said you looked in the mirror.

GOD. Oh, Jamie, don't you ever just lie? For fun?

JAMIE. Yeah, but...

GOD. I've got angels with sixteen fuckin eyes and not a one of them has ever looked me in the face. Too scared or it would be awkward or I don't know, they're really busy singing.

JAMIE. And so nobody ever –

GOD. Sees me. Including me.

I thought about it once and promised myself: hey, let's do this tomorrow.

Tomorrow came, and went, and now here I am. Like many centuries later.

I forgot, or. It was just easier to be busy.

JAMIE. I mean, I get it. We've all done it.

Is thiiiiis

(Gestures to all of **GOD***'s trappings and costume pieces.)*

what you want?

If you really want to be painted like a fluorescent glitter-bombed oil puddle, I'll do it.

GOD. Okay.

JAMIE. But it'll just be a glitter-bombed oil puddle.

I don't know if that's wrong or boring or both.

GOD. It might be.

JAMIE. It's a canvas, you know?

There will always be paint between you and its surface.

Between you and the world.

So...

GOD. Shhh, for fuck's sake. I need a minute.

JAMIE. Do you want –?

GOD. ZIP IT.

*(***GOD*** begins, with all the time it needs to take, the slow undoing of their raiment. Tusks are set aside. Jewels are carefully unwound. Marbles unhooked and bangles put aside.*

Tulle cloud puffs deflated. Whatever happens, happens. Slow and deliberate. Each piece means something different.)

*(At the end, **JAMIE** stands, and goes to the paint bucket. And **GOD** steps into the light, just as themself.)*

Should I pose?

JAMIE. No, I don't think so.

GOD. But *can* I?

JAMIE. If you want, but would you come closer?

*(**GOD** approaches. Their careful steps are not out of fear, but out of respect for each molecule and atom they touch. **JAMIE** dips the brush in the paint.)*

May I?

GOD. Yes.

*(**JAMIE** lifts the brush and gently paints **GOD**'s face in an even layer. They are thorough but not slow. They tilt their chin back and forth with a finger as needed. A soft hum begins in the background, almost musical.)*

*(The brush tickles **GOD**'s nose, and **GOD** giggles. Both of them smile for a moment.)*

*(When the painting is done, **JAMIE** takes **GOD** by the wrist and leads them to the canvas. **JAMIE** hesitates, an ask for permission, and **GOD** nods. They take **GOD**'s face in their hands and gently press it against the canvas: one side, and then the other.)*

(They step back.)

JAMIE. Look.

*(All the light focuses in, slowly, on the print of **GOD**'s face. Everything else fades away.)*

(All the creatures of the earth hum.)

Imposter's Eve^ZZZ

Malique Guinn

IMPOSTER'S EVE^{zzz} was first produced by Take Ten, a Virtual Ten Minute Play Festival on May 19th, 2022. The performance was directed by NJ Agwuna. The cast was as follows:

BRENT . . . . Esco Jouley

QUE . . . . Brandon Gill

CHARACTERS

BRENT – 19, Black.
QUE – 25, Black.

SETTING

Las Vegas. Hotel is "Circus Circus" adjacent.

AUTHOR'S NOTES

I encourage you to play with the ticking sound in relation to time. For example, each tick could represent a minute. Or three minutes. Or five. Have fun with it. Be childlike. God bless.

(Lights up on a standard hotel room.)

(Two queen beds. A dresser with a television on top and a desk in the corner.)

*(**QUE** and **BRENT** kneel in front of one with their hands folded.)*

QUE. And Lord, we come against imposter's syndrome. We know that you make no mistakes and your will is always done. We thank you Lord for safe travels and meetin' the desires of Brent by givin' him this new job opportunity in IT.

BRENT. Mmm.

QUE. With nice pay.

BRENT. Mmmmm.

QUE. And benefitssssss.

BRENT. MMMMMMM.

QUE. In Jesus name we pray, amen.

*(**BRENT** and **QUE** stand up and embrace.)*

BRENT. Thank you bro.

QUE. Let's count some sheep.

*(**BRENT** and **QUE** get into their beds and lie down.)*

(Silence.)

BRENT. Can you be a little quieter?

QUE. Huh?

BRENT. You gotta be quiet.

QUE. I didn't say nothin'.

BRENT. Okay.

> *(Silence. A loud ticking sound starts.)*

> *(**QUE** sits up and the sound stops.)*

QUE. The hell is that?!

BRENT. Ughhh I can't sleep.

QUE. You thinkin' 'bout it too much. Too damn excited is all.

BRENT. I know. I still can't believe it.

QUE. Well it's the real deal now bro. Real as a fossil.

BRENT. Okay let's try to be quiet again.

> *(**QUE** lays back down.)*

> *(Silence. The ticking sound starts again.)*

> *(**BRENT** sits up and the sound stops.)*

Oh my God! I can't sleep!

QUE. Dawg, you need to relax.

BRENT. I'm trying but I can't. I don't want to be late.

QUE. You won't be late bro. *(Takes out phone and shows* **BRENT**.*)* I have three alarms set. One at 4:30, 5, then 5:30.

BRENT. Will your alarm actually go off though?

QUE. I'm positive. And you have alarms set right?

BRENT. Yeah.

QUE. Alright then you'll be straight.

BRENT. Cool…let's try this again.

(**BRENT** *lies back down.*)

(*Silence. Once again, that freakin' ticking.*)

QUE. Fam! Is there a mouse in the room or somethin'?

BRENT. I can't keep my eyes closed.

QUE. Huh?!

BRENT. My eyes won't close, no matter how hard I try.

(**QUE** *sits up and faces* **BRENT.**)

QUE. Try to close your eyes.

(**BRENT***'s eyes flutter rapidly.*)

What the hell?!

BRENT. It's so weird!

QUE. What do they call that? REM, right?

BRENT. Yeah but that's when you're already sleep.

QUE. That's so weird.

BRENT. REM?

QUE. No, your eyes clickity clackin'.

BRENT. Let me just throw on my work fit.

QUE. It's gonna get wrinkled.

BRENT. I don't wanna be late Que.

(**BRENT** *gets up and retrieves cargo pants, a button up, and a jacket from his duffle bag. He puts them on.*)

Okay I should be good now.

QUE. You sure?

BRENT. I hope so.

> (**BRENT** *hops back into bed.*)
>
> (**QUE** *lies back down.*)
>
> (*Silence. And guess what happens? Ticking!*)
>
> (**QUE** *sits up.*)

QUE. Alright man you know what...

BRENT. I can't help it.

QUE. You're too damn excited bro.

BRENT. Alright I'll just go into the bathroom and –

QUE. AHT! AHT! No.

BRENT. It would help.

QUE. Touchin' yourself to sleep will not help.

BRENT. ...You think you can get me some Vicks? That usually helps me a lot.

QUE. *(Sighs.)* Sure.

> (**QUE** *gets out of bed and puts on his PJ pants. He exits the stage.*)
>
> (*Meanwhile,* **BRENT** *tries to sleep again.*)
>
> (*Tick. Tick. Tick.*)
>
> (**QUE** *enters stage with a thick jar of Vicks. He tosses it to* **BRENT.**)

Got enough Vicks to make an onion cry. Knock yourself out.

BRENT. Thanks.

QUE. So you gonna be straight now?

BRENT. I should be.

QUE. Smooth.

> (**QUE** *strips off his PJ pants and gets into bed.*)

> (**BRENT** *gets up and goes into the bathroom.*)

What are you doin'?

BRENT. I'm just rubbing the Vicks on my chest.

QUE. Alright, don't be rubbin' nothin' else.

BRENT. I won't.

QUE. My ears are sharp as snail teeth.

BRENT. I know.

> (**BRENT** *exits the bathroom. He sighs and hits his fist against the wall.*)

Oh my Goddddd!!

QUE. Bro what you do that for?!

BRENT. I can't sleep!!

QUE. Okay but you can't be hittin' the wall. I'm gonna get charged for that if there's damage.

> (**BRENT** *plops onto the bed.*)

> (**QUE** *gets up and sits at the desk.*)

You know what? I'll just sit here until you fall asleep. I got you.

BRENT. *(Groans.)* I can't lose this job Que. I wanted this really badly.

QUE. You won't bro.

BRENT. I don't wanna have to stay in Lancaster.

QUE. And you won't. This is the new chapter. Ain't no turnin' back.

BRENT. That's why I'm feeling so anxious. Que if I lose this job…

QUE. Like I said, everythin' will be fine.

BRENT. And I can't have caffeine, it's against my religion.

QUE. God forgave you for masturbatin'. He can forgive you for caffeine, especially since He brought you to this. He met your desires. Look at you. You're in Vegas, close to your concerts. Finally getting your own place.

BRENT. I know. It's still so surreal to me. I'm very grateful. I didn't think I'd even be alive for this.

QUE. …We're all proud of you bro, forreal. They're gonna be glad to have you in the building.

BRENT. I just still doubt myself. Like it feels like a mistake. I know it's not, but it'll just take me some time to not think like that.

QUE. Let me just say this. It don't matter what I say about you. Don't forget who God says you are. And that's for damn sure not an imposter. The favor on your life is unlike anythin' you could imagine. This is only the beginnin'. You had your trials. I had my trials. Mom and Dad had their trials. Yet and still, here we are. God has kept us in spite of it all.

BRENT. Thank you Que. I'm so glad you're my brother.

QUE. Likewise. Wouldn't want it any other way. Hell, you inspire me.

> (**BRENT** *goes over to* **QUE** *and embraces him tightly.*)

I love you so much bro.

BRENT. I love you too.

QUE. You're gonna be amazin'.

BRENT. As long as I get some sleep.

QUE. Yeeaaaaah, what time is it anyway? *(Pulls out phone.)* Oh damn. 11:25.

> *(**BRENT** dashes to the bed.)*

You got your phone on the charger right?

BRENT. Yup.

QUE. Cool. I'll still sit here until you knock out.

BRENT. Sounds good.

> *(**BRENT** gets under the covers.)*

> *(Ticking sound starts again.)*

QUE. *(Singing.*)*
READY FOR WARRRRRR, READY FOR BATTLEEEEEE, READY FOR BLESSINGSSSSSSS, READY FOR CATTLEEEEEE.

> *(Ticking slows, matching **QUE**'s singing as he drifts away into slumber.)*

(Singing.)
WE GIVE UNTO GODDDDD, WHAT WE CANNOT HANDLEEEEEE, NEVER IMPOSTERSSSSS, THE LIES ARE DISMANTLED.

> *(The ticking slows down even more. It continues to slow as **QUE**'s singing fades out.)*

> *(The ticking stops.)*

> *(Them boys are finally knocked out.)*

---

* A license to produce *Imposter's Eve*^{ZZZ} does not include a performance license for any third-party or copyrighted music. Licensees should create an original composition or use music in the public domain. For further information, please see the Music and Third-Party Materials Use Note on page iii.

...in daylight

DJ Hills

...in daylight was first produced by Take Ten, a Virtual Ten Minute Play Festival on May 19th, 2022. The performance was directed by victor cervantes jr. The cast was as follows:

SABINE . . . . Pooya Mosheni

LEO. . . . . Bradley Tejeda

CHARACTERS

SABINE – she/her/hers – early forties

LEO – he/him/his – late twenties – a slight accent of indeterminate origins

SETTING

A hilltop outside of a small village in a very northern country.

TIME

July, this year

(darkness
movement in the darkness
the movement stops)

LEO. we should go up a little higher

SABINE. if we keep walking we're going to miss it

LEO. i don't think that's possible

SABINE. let's just stop

please

leo

we're high enough

LEO. okay
> *(darkness still*
> *a pinprick of light somewhere)*

SABINE. i've never been up this high

the town looks so small

LEO. just wait

once the sun comes up everyone turns off all the lights

SABINE. seven minute

wait a whole year for seven minutes

okay

let's do it
> *(more light*
> *we're beginning to see them now*
> *they turn their backs to one another and*
> *undress)*

SABINE. well

LEO. well

SABINE. it's cold

like really fucking cold

> *(they laugh*
> *they are standing in their underwear*
> **LEO** *turns around)*

but not

not as cold as i thought it would be

it's never as cold as i think it should be

LEO. it's the river

all the water coming in from the ocean

> *(he's guessing now:)*

the underground geysers

something about the climate

SABINE. you don't know

LEO. *(laughs)*

i guess i don't pay enough attention

SABINE. huh

okay i'm ready

> *(she turns around)*

oh

LEO. what?

SABINE. you're

LEO. my??

SABINE. no no you're

you're
> *(she places a hand on his chest*
> *she touches his chest*
> *she touches his stomach*
> *she touches his mouth*
> *she touches his throat)*

interesting
> *(**LEO** takes both of her hands*
> *he blows on her fingers and then*
> *he moves her hands toward his crotch*
> ***SABINE** pulls away*
> *she smacks his shoulder*
> *they laugh*
> *she looks around*
> *she shivers)*

let's get dressed
> *(she turns back to **LEO***
> *he is about to take off his underwear)*

LEO. oh uh

SABINE. oh unless

LEO. i thought

no okay let's

SABINE. i mean it's kind of

LEO. sure sure

i just thought

SABINE. right

LEO. you'd said

SABINE. but now i

i mean i've seen it before

LEO. oh

yeah

SABINE. *(laughs)* no not that

it's just

LEO. no it's okay let's

SABINE. i just mean i feel like i've seen your best parts already

(beat)

LEO. right

(**LEO** *gets dressed*)

SABINE. not that your

i'm

i meant it *romantically*

LEO. sure sure

SABINE. leo

(**LEO** *hands her coat*
kisses her
smiles)

LEO. it's fine

i'm not

don't worry

(they finish getting dressed
it is fully light now

> *for a moment their surroundings open up*
> *around them)*

we don't have much longer

SABINE. i thought you said we had seven minutes

LEO. i did

SABINE. how long has it been?

LEO. i wasn't counting

two minutes? three?

SABINE. well now what do we do?

LEO. i don't know

make a wish?

> *(they stand still for a moment*
> *then:* **SABINE** *closes her eyes*
> **LEO** *watches and then closes his eyes*
> *they wish*
> **LEO** *opens his eyes*
> **SABINE** *is still wishing*
> *beat)*

LEO. so what

SABINE. wait

> **(LEO** *waits*
> *pause then:)*

LEO. it's already getting darker

> *(and so it is*
> **SABINE** *opens her eyes)*

what did you wish for?

SABINE. i can't tell you

LEO. why not?

SABINE. then it won't come true

LEO. why not?

SABINE. what did *you* wish for?

LEO. this

SABINE. *this??*

      (she looks around)

LEO. us i meant

us this

us together

i wished for

us

SABINE. oh

LEO. i saw us

living together

somewhere

here??

with kids and

SABINE. *(laughs)*

leo i'm not

i don't want kids

LEO. just listen

i had this

vision

stop don't laugh

i had a thought

i saw

it was a monday and you were leaving to teach class and you were late and one of the kids the youngest *stop* was crying because she hadn't been fed yet and you were trying to warm up a bottle but the cap came off and it spilled

    (he touches just under her collar bone)

and there was

this little red mark from the warm milk

and

and it was

    (he traces out the shape over her coat)

a little red mark

    (he blows on her neck)

    (beat)

SABINE. so your wish was for me to get covered in formula?

some fetish i don't know about?

LEO. sabine

SABINE. i'm sorry

i'm not

it was very

that's very sweet

LEO. what about you?

SABINE. oh i wished there was a starbucks up here

LEO. sab

SABINE. i didn't wish for anything

i just

listened

> *(she closes her eyes)*

you know i think the sun has a very particular sound

i didn't notice it before i came here but if you

the air

sounds different

it sounds

.

.

.

> *(she opens her eyes*
> **LEO** *has kept his eyes open)*

what?

LEO. you're pretty

SABINE. i know

> *(**LEO** laughs)*

when i was living in anchorage i was dating this woman

ursula

she was a graduate student

not my department

she told me alaska has this obscene rate of sexual
assault

more than anywhere else in the united states

she was studying it

she thought it had something to do with the darkness

all the night how long it is

i was always safe but

after she told me that i

i bought locks

i bought so many locks

it was stupid how many locks i bought

and i didn't do anything with them

i'd find them

in the oddest places around the apartment

in drawers and under magazines

i started treating them like totems

like if i found a lock that morning i was safe for the rest
of the day

i don't know

and then i read about this place

in *the new yorker*

this

this odd little space in the world where the sun shines
for exactly seven minutes

every year

and i

i needed

i don't know

to prove something?

are you ever afraid?

LEO. of? darkness?

sure

SABINE. but not

LEO. maybe it's different

growing up here

SABINE. maybe

(pause
the light is dim)

i think

living in darkness

i think it

does something to a person

LEO. you know this isn't

i've seen the sun

i've been places before

toronto and

SABINE. i know

LEO. i'm not a

a hermit or

some feral animal

SABINE. of course

i wasn't

i know

LEO. do you?

(beat)

SABINE. i'm not going to stay here forever

i want

i never wanted that

LEO. yes i

wait

are?

i'm sorry

are you

breaking up??

with me

SABINE. no

do you want me to?

LEO. *no*

SABINE. okay

LEO. "okay"???

(the light is dimmer)

SABINE. i forget that you're a man sometimes

i know that sounds stupid but

i mean i *know*

but

sometimes

when i left alaska i was so numb

just *worn down* from

from all the

the worrying i guess

the

SABINE. and after being here a while i just

    sort of forgot

    i forgot everything

    anchorage and

    and everything

    i would wake up and go teach and come home and day
    after day every minute

    just this

    this same

    darkness

    this same anxiousness

    i think i got used to it

    i felt so detached from everyone

    from my body

    i kept waiting

    waiting for

    for something

    and then

    i went into the hardware store for i don't remember

    hardware?

    and i saw you

    and you were holding a lock

    just a normal padlock

    and i felt this

    you know you have the *strangest neck*

    it's so

(she makes a gesture
a clasp of hands around nothing)

i saw you and i just wanted to wrap my hands around it and

dig out your throat

because you were *hard*

(laughs)

grounded i mean

real??

and i wasn't exhausted or anxious or afraid

i was just

mad

i was so mad at you

(pause
it is almost completely dark now)

LEO. i don't know what to say to that

SABINE. i don't need you to say anything

LEO. i'm not going to hurt you sab

(pause
a pinprick of light growing fainter)

SABINE. but you could

(silence
LEO *steps forward*
he holds her head between his hands
he goes to kiss her
darkness
silence)

LEO. sabine?

    (silence)

sleepover

Alica Daine Benning

sleepover was first produced by Take Ten, a Virtual Ten Minute Play Festival on May 19th, 2022. The performance was directed by Jessica Holt The cast was as follows:

ANI . . . . .Aizzah Fatima
BEATRICE . . . . .Shelly Safir Marolt

CHARACTERS

ANI
BEATRICE

SETTING

an ambiguous living room. or maybe someplace else.

TIME

present day.

AUTHOR'S NOTES

please cast people of all genders, ages, races and ethnicities to play these roles.
the play is open-ended. please be daring.

(two girls sitting at opposite ends of a couch.)

(they sit in lightly uncomfortable silence for a beat.)

ANI. would you like a drink?

BEATRICE. what kind of drink?

ANI. what would you like?

BEATRICE. what do you have?

ANI. water, soda, juice...

BEATRICE. what kind of juice?

ANI. cranberry, apple, lime...

*(a beat. **BEATRICE** considers.)*

BEATRICE. you have lime juice?

ANI. yes.

BEATRICE. why?

ANI. for cocktails.

BEATRICE. you didn't offer me a cocktail.

ANI. we're not old enough for cocktails.

BEATRICE. aren't we?

ANI. of course not.

(a beat.)

would you like a cocktail?

BEATRICE. no.

(*a beat.*)

ANI. why are we here again?

BEATRICE. we are having a sleepover.

ANI. oh.

BEATRICE. it is supposed to be very fun.

ANI. okay. what should we do?

BEATRICE. we could do a face mask. we could put on a white strip. we could dance around in our underwear and have a pillow fight.

ANI. i don't want to do that.

(*a beat.*)

what if we talk about our feelings?

BEATRICE. i don't want to do that.

ANI. are you afraid?

BEATRICE. no.

ANI. you are.

(*a beat.*)

BEATRICE. fine. i'm afraid.

ANI. why?

BEATRICE. i don't know.

i don't know my own feelings.

ANI. that's okay.

BEATRICE. no it's not. it's bad.

(*a beat.*)

ANI. how do you feel?

BEATRICE. stop it.

ANI. how do you feel!

BEATRICE. stop it!

ANI. tell me how you feel!

BEATRICE. about what!

ANI. about anything!

BEATRICE. like??

ANI. about me!

BEATRICE. no.

ANI. about yourself then.

BEATRICE. also no.

ANI. i can go first.

BEATRICE. fine. whatever.

ANI. i love you.

(a beat.)

BEATRICE. what?

ANI. you heard me!

BEATRICE. no.

ANI. i love you.

BEATRICE. you do not.

ANI. yes i do.

BEATRICE. no you don't!

ANI. you can't argue with me about how i feel.

BEATRICE. yes i can. of course i can.

ANI. i love you!

BEATRICE. no you don't!

ANI. yes i do!

BEATRICE. i hate you.

ANI. fine.

> *(a beat.)*

really?

BEATRICE. shut up.

> *(a beat.)*

ANI. what do people do at sleepovers.

BEATRICE. i don't know. i think just self-improvement stuff.

ANI. like face masks?

BEATRICE. yeah. or nails.

or we could highlight our hair.

ANI. how would we do that?

BEATRICE. we could to go to albertson's

ANI. we can't drive

BEATRICE. well we could get your mom to go to albertson's

ANI. my mom shops at safeway

BEATRICE. and buy a kit.

ANI. what kind of kit?

BEATRICE. a hair striper kit.

ANI. hair...striper?

BEATRICE. yes. for putting stripes in your hair.

ANI. i don't know if i want stripes in my hair.

BEATRICE. why not?

ANI. i like my hair how it is.

BEATRICE. i think your hair looks stupid.

ANI. that's not very nice.

BEATRICE. well, i'm not very nice.

ANI. you're very negative.

BEATRICE. well, that's just the way i am.

ANI. well, i wish you were different.

BEATRICE. well, how come you <u>love</u> me so much if all you want to do is change me!

ANI. i don't want to change you! i just want you to be, different.

BEATRICE. different how.

ANI. less negative.

BEATRICE. well, that's the way i am, and a tiger can't change its stripes.

ANI. what does that mean?

BEATRICE. i don't know. my mom always says it.

ANI. well, it's negative.

BEATRICE. shut up shut up shut up.

ANI. i wish you'd be kind to yourself. i wish you'd give yourself love.

BEATRICE. why would anybody need to do that.

ANI. because it feels good.

BEATRICE. yeah, right.

ANI. better than hating yourself.

BEATRICE. i never said i hated myself!

ANI. oh.

BEATRICE. i said i hated you.

ANI. okay.

BEATRICE. don't misquote me.

ANI. well, that's still very negative.

BEATRICE. you're so judgmental.

ANI. i don't think so.

BEATRICE. well, i do.

ANI. well, i don't!

BEATRICE. fine!

(a long beat.)

ANI. are you me?

BEATRICE. are you me?

ANI. are we each other?

BEATRICE. i don't know.

ANI. are you my mother?

BEATRICE. i don't want to be.

ANI. i don't want you to be.

(a beat.)

BEATRICE. i don't claim you.

ANI. that's okay.

BEATRICE. you don't care that i don't claim you?

ANI. i claim myself.

BEATRICE. that's stupid.

(a beat.)

your boobs are too small.

ANI. okay.

BEATRICE. your skin is uneven.

ANI. okay.

BEATRICE. your lips are too thin.

ANI. okay.

BEATRICE. your interests are silly.

ANI. okay.

BEATRICE. i don't like your outfit.

ANI. okay.

BEATRICE. your feet are too big.

ANI. this is <u>exhausting</u>.

BEATRICE. you'll never find love.

ANI. yes i will!

BEATRICE. all your friends hate you.

everyone hates you.

ANI. do you hate me?

(a beat.)

are you my friend?

(a beat.)

BEATRICE. how can you ask me that?

ANI. answer the question.

BEATRICE. i am your <u>best</u> friend.

ANI. you are my <u>worst</u> friend.

(a beat.)

i wish you could be kind to me.

(a beat.)

BEATRICE. i do, too.

ANI. you are my best friend.

BEATRICE. i know.

ANI. you are my <u>best friend.</u>

BEATRICE. i <u>know.</u>

(*a beat.*)

ANI. should we do something sleepover-y?

BEATRICE. like what?

ANI. i don't know.

BEATRICE. manicures? white strips?

ANI. i don't really want to do anything that alters my appearance.

BEATRICE. fine.

(*a beat.*)

ANI. do boys have sleepovers?

BEATRICE. i don't know.

ANI. we should ask one.

BEATRICE. probably they wouldn't tell us.

ANI. i want to know what boys do at sleepovers.

BEATRICE. probably nothing.

ANI. nothing?

BEATRICE. probably sports.

ANI. do you think they do face masks and put stripes in their hair?

BEATRICE. no, i don't.

ANI. do you think they talk about their feelings?

BEATRICE. i don't know.

ANI. well, what do you think?

BEATRICE. i don't know.

ANI. fine.

(*a beat.*)

BEATRICE. if they did, i doubt they'd tell us.

(*a beat.*)

ANI. can i tell you something

BEATRICE. what

ANI. can i or not

BEATRICE. fine, sure

ANI. i am grateful for you.

(*a beat.*)

BEATRICE. you are?

ANI. yes.

(*a beat.*)

ANI. i don't know what i would do without you.

BEATRICE. me neither.

ANI. i don't know who i would be.

BEATRICE. neither do i.

(*a beat.*)

(*the girls sit in silence.*)

(**BEATRICE** *pulls a bottle of nail polish out of her pocket, begins to paint her nails.*)

(**ANI** *watches, mesmerized.*)

ANI. will you do mine?

BEATRICE. really?

ANI. yes.

BEATRICE. i thought you didn't want to.

ANI. i changed my mind.

>　　*(a beat.)*

BEATRICE. okay.

>　　*(**BEATRICE** begins to paint **ANI**'s nails.)*

>　　*(a beat in silence.)*

The Death Card

Forest Malley

THE DEATH CARD was first produced by Take Ten, a Virtual Ten Minute Play Festival on May 19th, 2022. The performance was directed by NJ Agwuna. The cast was as follows:

VIRGO GIRL. . . . . .Aizzah Fatima
TAURUS GUY. . . . . Bradley Tejeda

CHARACTERS

VIRGO GIRL – (Abbreviated "Virgo") – f., twenties, a spiritual hack. She
really wants to see other people.

TAURUS GUY – (Abbreviated "Taurus") – m., twenties, a bit of a jackass.
He is already seeing other people.

(*At rise,* **VIRGO GIRL** *is arranging the seating space. Maybe she throws a pillow or a blanket down, lights a candle, waves something in the air to cleanse the space. She stops for a moment, admiring her work.*)

(**TAURUS GUY** *enters, apprehensive.*)

VIRGO GIRL. Oh, there you are babe! I'm almost ready.

TAURUS GUY. Here I am. Should I keep my shoes on?

VIRGO GIRL. What do you mean?

TAURUS GUY. Like I don't know, like with yoga. Will it help with the reading?

VIRGO GIRL. Will it help me read your tarot cards if you take your shoes off?

(*They look at each other.* **TAURUS GUY** *really can't tell if she's being sarcastic. He takes off his shoes.*)

TAURUS GUY. Can you explain this whole thing to me again?

(**VIRGO GIRL** *sits cross-legged across from him and pulls out the tarot cards, spreading them across the table.*)

VIRGO GIRL. I'm going to connect with your energy, and then I'm going to connect with Spirit, and then I'm going to do your reading based on what the cards tell me.

TAURUS. So you're going to read my mind?

VIRGO. The cards are going to read your energy, and I'm going to read the cards.

>   *(Off his confused look.)*

Yeah, sure, I'm going to read your mind.

TAURUS. Will you like...like be able to see things I haven't told you?

VIRGO. What haven't you told me?

TAURUS. I don't know. Stuff. Private stuff.

VIRGO. Nothing is private in tarot.

TAURUS. Fuck.

VIRGO. Just sit down.

>   *(He sits.)*

Okay. As a Virgo, obviously, I have a really intuitive nature. I'm very observant. So this should be easy, I can feel a lot of your energy already. Can you close your eyes for me?

TAURUS. Okay.

>   *(He closes his eyes. **VIRGO** makes the quietest possible gesture to communicate that she hates his guts, and then takes a deep breath.)*

VIRGO. Are you breathing with me?

TAURUS. Oh, no, I wasn't. Well I was breathing, but not with you. Or – I'm with you, I just wasn't breathing with you.

I'll do it now.

>   *(They breathe for a second.)*

VIRGO. *(Eyes still closed, sniffing.)* Did you shower after the gym?

TAURUS. I washed my hands.

VIRGO. Did you wash your body?

TAURUS. I thought about it for sure.

VIRGO. Let's just skip breathing. Open your eyes.

(*She shuffles the deck and pulls eight random cards. She makes an exaggerated gasp.*)

TAURUS. What, what do you see? Is it bad?

VIRGO. It's – let's just work through it together.

TAURUS. Oh fuck.

VIRGO. Okay, right off the bat. This card (*Any random card.*) tells me you're...um...you're such a great guy. A classic Taurus. Loyal, kind, you've been so good to me.

TAURUS. Aww, babe.

VIRGO. ...and like, um, my mother likes you –

TAURUS. She does?

VIRGO. Sure.

TAURUS. It says that on the card?

VIRGO. Word for word, yeah.

TAURUS. Sick.

VIRGO. The point is, the card wants to start off by saying, no matter what happens in this reading, you're a standup guy. Like, that time you let me vomit in your backpack at Six Flags? That was so chivalrous.

TAURUS. Wow. I do sound like a really good guy. I fuck with tarot.

VIRGO. Alright whatever. See this?

(*She pulls a random card.*)

VIRGO. This tells me...things aren't as they seem. And they're in flux. Does that resonate?

TAURUS. I don't know. How would I know?

VIRGO. It would feel right. Does it feel right?

TAURUS. I think...I think things are as they seem, I guess.

VIRGO. Interesting.

(She picks up another card.).

This card tells me that...there's a situation in your life. A stable, permanent one. Its vibrancy might be starting to fade, does that make sense? Like, not everyone involved in the situation feels the same fire, the same desire, the same vitality. It also tells me that you haven't communicated about this yet with this person, but that they might have been feeling this way for a while. Like, I don't know, since last February. Possibly due to poor communication. And I don't know. Vibes.

TAURUS. You can see all of that in that card?

VIRGO. Yes. It's the...

(Checks the card.)

Ace of Swords. Classic Ace of Swords message.

TAURUS. Okay.

VIRGO. Whenever I see the Ace of Swords it makes me think – someone's not telling the whole truth, you know? And those truths need to come to light.

TAURUS. *(Squirming.)* Does it get any more specific than that? Or is that all you can see?

VIRGO. That's all for now.

TAURUS. *(A little relieved.)* Alright. We can stop here, honestly, I found out I'm a great guy, your mom loves me –

VIRGO. Likes you.

TAURUS. Likes me, yeah, I think this has been a great reading.

(He moves to stand up.)

VIRGO. Hold on, hold on, we're almost done.

(Beat.)

Do you...do you see where the cards are leading you?

TAURUS. Not exactly.

VIRGO. Okay, let's try another card... *(She pulls at random.)* Mmm, the death card.

TAURUS. Jesus.

VIRGO. Okay, it's not necessarily what you think.

TAURUS. You mean it's not like I'm gonna fucking die?

VIRGO. It might signify that something else has died. Like, a spark. Or, I don't know, that it's time to make way for *new* people, new situations, let go of the old.

TAURUS. Are you sure that doesn't just mean I'm gonna die.

VIRGO. Yes I'm fucking sure, I'm the one who knows about astrology. You're the one asking if wearing your shoes will affect the reading.

TAURUS. Okay, okay, sorry. Damn.

VIRGO. No, I'm sorry. I know this can be overwhelming. Let me see if I can put it differently –

TAURUS. Can I ask a question?

VIRGO. Yeah.

TAURUS. When you say let go of old situations, bring in the new. Could that be...something that already happened, or is it always what's going to happen?

VIRGO. What do you mean?

TAURUS. *(Nervously.)* Like, do the cards know...do they know what happened in the past?

VIRGO. The cards aren't sentient.

TAURUS. But, do you know what happened? In the past? By looking at the cards?

VIRGO. *(Shrugging.)* I know a lot of things.

TAURUS. I didn't kill anything.

VIRGO. I'm just telling you what the cards say. And the cards say something in your life is...it's time to *change* something in your life, because it's dying. Who's to say if you're the one who killed it or not.

> *(Thinking out loud.)*

I mean, I don't know, sometimes I think it was me...

TAURUS. I need some water. Or some food, I'm feeling light headed.

> **(TAURUS** *is freaked out, so he stands up.)*

VIRGO. Again, CLASSIC TAURUS!

TAURUS. I don't know if I'm comfortable with this. I don't know, I don't like you up there, I don't like you in my head.

VIRGO. I'm not in your head, what are you talking about? I'm reading the cards. The cards are in your head.

TAURUS. You just said the cards aren't sentient!

VIRGO. *(Smiling.)* I did say that, didn't I.

TAURUS. Besides, this is all bullshit. It's just – it's random, it's chance.

VIRGO. If that's how you see it.

TAURUS. Stop talking like that! Jesus, you're giving me chest pain.

VIRGO. Very fearful avoidant of you.

TAURUS. *(He's clutching his chest dramatically.)* I don't know, I feel like you have something to say. But I didn't do anything! I didn't kill anyone, or anything, I'm just a guy. Whatever you think you see, whatever you think you know, I don't know anything about that.

> *(**VIRGO** is a little confused. She's really just trying to fuck other people.)*

VIRGO. I really don't know why you're being so dramatic about this. It's just a tarot reading.

TAURUS. Because! Because I feel like you're accusing me of something, and I don't like that you can – I don't like that you can see all my thoughts and all my feelings.

VIRGO. I'm not accusing you of anything.

TAURUS. It was one fucking time! One time, it didn't mean anything, I don't even remember it that well, you're the one making it into some big thing – we barely even did anything, I was just fucked up!

> *(**VIRGO** gets it now. At first she's a little shocked but then she starts to laugh a little.)*

Why are you *LAUGHING?!*

VIRGO. Nothing, it's really nothing. Ummm...what am I supposed to ask...what's her name?

TAURUS. I don't know. I don't remember.

VIRGO. What's her sign?

TAURUS. How should I know? God, why are you even –

VIRGO. Is she a Scorpio? It's giving Scorpio.

TAURUS. I just said I don't know.

VIRGO. Let's just pull one more card, okay? Then we can be done with this whole little adventure.

TAURUS. *(Pacing.)* Jesus.

VIRGO. Mmm. Yeah. Makes sense.

TAURUS. What, what now.

VIRGO. *(Shrugging.)* It says we should see other people. Damn.

TAURUS. What?

VIRGO. The card, it says we should see other people. I mean, I wasn't thinking this before the reading necessarily, but with everything that just came to light – god, how crazy. Everything can change in an instant.

TAURUS. I don't wanna see other people.

VIRGO. There's a lot of cosmic energy telling me that this is what has to happen.

TAURUS. We don't have to do what the cards tell us.

VIRGO. Are you really asking me to turn my back on Spirit? On my entire belief system?

> *(A little beat.)*

TAURUS. Does it really say we should break up?

VIRGO. I mean, this combined with the other cards – it's curtains, my friend.

> *(She stands up and puts a hand on his shoulder.)*

I think this has been really good for us.

> *(She starts to walk offstage. On her exit:)*

Oh, yeah. The death card can also mean you're about to die. I just don't like to tell people that, it tends to freak them out.

(Scene.)

www.ingramcontent.com/pod-product-compliance
Lightning Source LLC
Chambersburg PA
CBHW070332120726
47909CB00008B/2678